HI,
WORD BIRD!

by Jane Belk Moncure
illustrated by Linda Sommers Hohag

THE CHILD'S WORLD

Library of Congress Cataloging in Publication Data

Moncure, Jane Belk.
  Hi, Word Bird!

  (Her Word Birds for Early Birds)
  Summary: Uses a very simple vocabulary to follow
Word Bird as he hatches and learns to hop, jump,
swim, and fly.
  [1. Birds—Fiction] I. Hohag, Linda Sommers.
II. Title. III. Series: Moncure, Jane Belk.
Early bird reader.
PZ7.M739Hi [E] 80-15919
ISBN 0-89565-159-9 (Child's World)

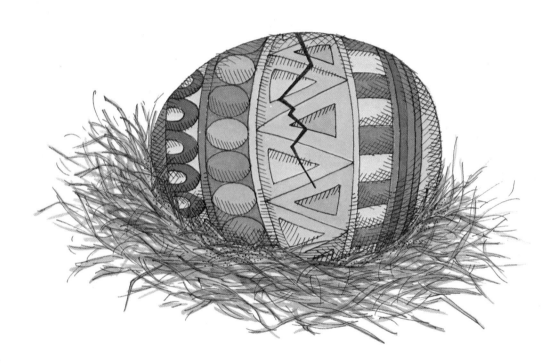

Pop.

Hi, Word Bird.

Cherry.

Cherry. Cherry.

Hop.

Hop, hop.

Jump.

Jump, jump.

Up.

Up, up.

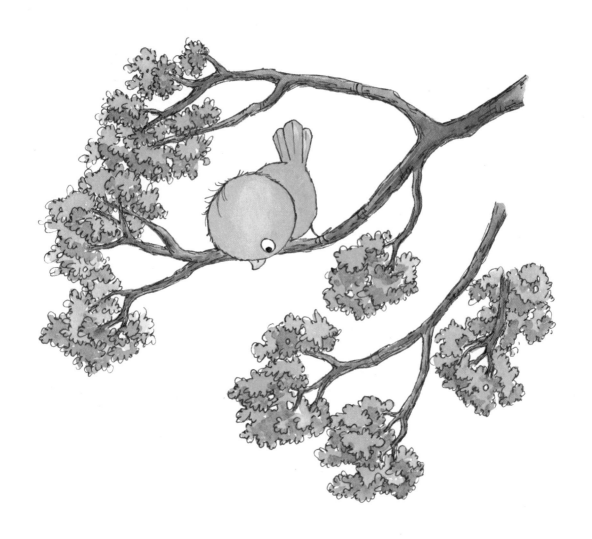

Down.

14

Down,
down.

In.

In, in.

Swim down.

Swim down.

Swim up.

Swim up.

Out.

Out, out.

Wet.

Dry.

Hi.

Hi.

Fly.

Fly. Fly.

Bye-bye.

You can read these  words.

pop

hi

up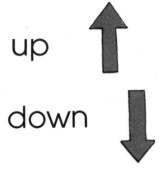

down

cherry

in

out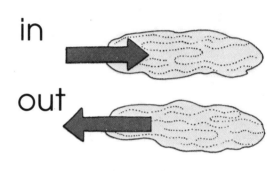

hop

swim

jump

bye-bye

fly